EURYDICE

PERSEUS

CASSIOPEIA

ORION

INTRODUCTION

THOUSANDS OF YEARS AGO, THE STARS PROVIDED KEY INFORMATION ABOUT THE WORLD. PATTERNS WERE IDENTIFIED, SO THAT THE STARS COULD BE USED FOR NAVIGATION, AS A CALENDAR AND AS A MEANS OF WORKING OUT WHEN TO PLANT CROPS AND WHEN TO HARVEST THEM. THE ANCIENT GREEKS PROJECTED STORIES OF THEIR GODS AND HEROES ONTO THESE PATTERNS, WHICH, LIKE THE GODS THEMSELVES, OFFERED SOME EXPLANATION FOR THE UNCERTAINTIES OF LIFE.

WHILST WE NOW KNOW THESE GROUPINGS OF STARS ARE RANDOM, THEY STILL PROVIDE US WITH A VALUABLE WAY OF ORIENTING OURSELVES IN THE UNIVERSE. EACH NIGHT A PROCESSION OF GREEK HEROES PARADES ACROSS THE SKY: CALLISTO ESCAPES HER HUNTERS, PEGASUS BATTLES THE CHIMERA AND ORION FLEES A GIANT SCORPION.

AND SO THE MYTHS OF THE GREEKS LIVE ON, HUNDREDS OF GENERATIONS LATER. AS THE STARS LIGHT OUR PRESENT, THEY CONTINUE TO ILLUMINATE THEIR PAST.

PEGASUS 10

OPHIUCUS
(THE SERPENT BEARER) 22

URSA MAJOR
(THE GREAT BEAR) 4

CORONA BOREALIS
(NORTHERN CROWN) 14

LYRE
(THE LYRE) 12

ANDROMEDA 6

HERCULES 8

ORION AND SCORPIUS 16

CENTAURUS
(THE CENTAUR) 20

CORVUS
(THE CROW) 18

CALLISTO IS SEDUCED BY ZEUS AND MUST HIDE THE RESULTING PREGNANCY FROM HER BELOVED ARTEMIS.

ENRAGED BY THE DECEPTION, ARTEMIS USES HER MIGHTY POWERS TO TRANSFORM CALLISTO INTO A BEAR.

CALLISTO WORSHIPS ARTEMIS, AND THE GODDESS REWARDS HER DEVOTION.

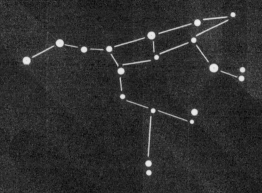

URSA MAJOR
(THE GREAT BEAR)

BEAUTIFUL CALLISTO, PRINCESS OF ARCADIA, WORSHIPPED ARTEMIS, GODDESS OF THE HUNT, BECOMING ONE OF HER NYMPHS AND TAKING A VOW OF CHASTITY. RECOGNISING HER DEVOTION AND HUNTING SKILLS, ARTEMIS MADE CALLISTO HER FAVOURITE COMPANION.

CALLISTO ALSO CAUGHT THE EYE OF ZEUS, WHO CAME TO THE FOREST DISGUISED AS ARTEMIS AND SEDUCED HER, LATER REVEALING HIS TRUE SELF. CALLISTO BECAME PREGNANT, BUT FOR MONTHS HID HER SWELLING SHAPE FROM THE GODDESS. FINALLY, STUMBLING IN THE CHASE, CALLISTO CONFESSED THE TRUTH.

FURIOUS AT THIS BETRAYAL, ARTEMIS THREW DOWN HER BOW AND STOOD OVER THE COWERING GIRL, RAISING HER ARMS IN RAGE. CALLISTO'S RICH RED HAIR TUMBLED OVER HER SHOULDERS, THICKENING INTO DEEP FUR. HER DELICATE HANDS CURLED INTO VICIOUS CLAWS AND HER SOBS DEEPENED INTO GUTTURAL GROWLS. THE HUNTRESS BECAME THE HUNTED; CALLISTO FLED FROM ARTEMIS IN THE FORM OF A BEAR.

ARETMIS AND HER FOLLOWERS PURSUED THE BEAST TO THE EDGE OF THE FOREST WHERE ITS TERRIFIED CRIES ECHOED TO THE HEAVENS. ZEUS HEARD AND TOOK PITY. AS ARTEMIS STRUNG HER BOW TO SHOOT, HE LIFTED THE BEAR FAR OUT OF REACH, CASTING HER IMAGE INTO THE STARS; URSA MAJOR.

ZEUS WITNESSES THE HUNT AND TAKES PITY, RESCUING CALLISTO AND PLACING HER FAR OUT OF REACH AMONGST THE STARS.

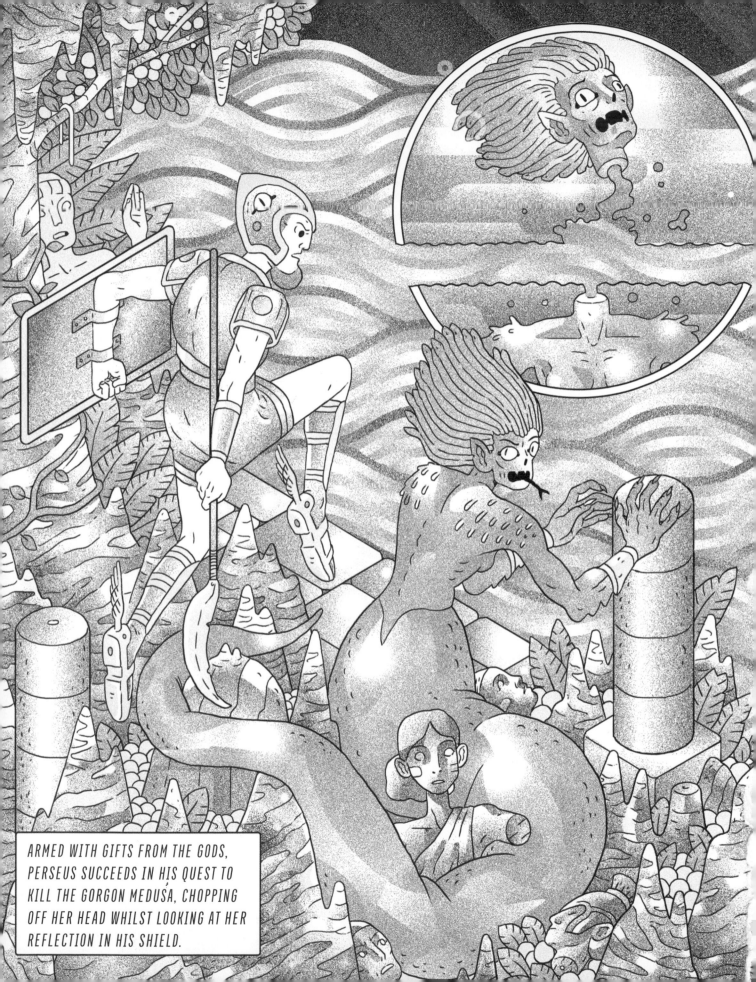

ARMED WITH GIFTS FROM THE GODS, PERSEUS SUCCEEDS IN HIS QUEST TO KILL THE GORGON MEDUSA, CHOPPING OFF HER HEAD WHILST LOOKING AT HER REFLECTION IN HIS SHIELD.

ANDROMEDA

THE GORGON MEDUSA WAS SO TERRIFYINGLY HIDEOUS THAT A SINGLE GLANCE FROM HER WOULD TURN MEN TO STONE. ONLY BRAVE PERSEUS WAS WILLING TO ACCEPT THE CHALLENGE OF KILLING THE GORGON. USING THE GIFTS OF THE GODS; A CLOAK OF INVISIBILITY FROM HADES, ATHENA'S BRONZE SHIELD AND ZEUS'S SWORD, PERSEUS SUCCEEDED IN HIS MISSION, LOOKING AT A REFLECTION OF THE GORGON IN HIS SHIELD BEFORE CHOPPING OFF HER HEAD.

WEARING HERMES'S WINGED SANDALS, PERSEUS FLEW HOMEWARDS. ON HIS WAY, A GLINT OF METAL ON A CLIFF FACE CAUGHT HIS EYE. BOUND BY CHAINS TO THE ROCKS, A YOUNG WOMAN TWISTED HELPLESSLY ABOVE THE CHURNING WAVES. THIS WAS ANDROMEDA, DAUGHTER OF QUEEN CASSIOPEIA, WHOSE VAIN BOAST THAT SHE WAS MORE BEAUTIFUL THAN ANY SEA NYMPH HAD ENRAGED THE SEA GOD POSEIDON. TREMBLING WITH FEAR, ANDROMEDA TOLD HER STORY TO PERSEUS; TO APPEASE POSEIDON, THE PRIESTS HAD ORDERED THE QUEEN TO SACRIFICE HER DAUGHTER. THUS, AS THE SILENT CROWDS STARED, ANDROMEDA AWAITED THE JAWS OF THE TERRIBLE SEA SERPENT, KRAKEN.

A GASP ABOVE ANNOUNCED THE MONSTER'S ARRIVAL. AS THE REPTILIAN SCALES AND SLASHING TEETH WRITHED UPWARDS, PERSEUS'S SWORD SLICED DOWNWARDS, AND THE SHUDDERING BODY OF THE MONSTER SANK BACK BENEATH THE WAVES.

HEROIC ONCE MORE, PERSEUS CLAIMED ANDROMEDA AS HIS WIFE. BLESSED BY THE GODS, THE COUPLE LIVED HAPPILY, THEIR CHILDREN THE FORBEARERS OF BOTH PERSIA AND SPARTA. TO COMMEMORATE THEIR LIVES, THE GODDESS ATHENA CAST THEIR IMAGE INTO THE STARS. ANDROMEDA LIES BETWEEN CASSIOPEIA, THE MOTHER WHO SACRIFICED HER LOVE, AND PERSEUS, THE ONE WHO CLAIMED IT.

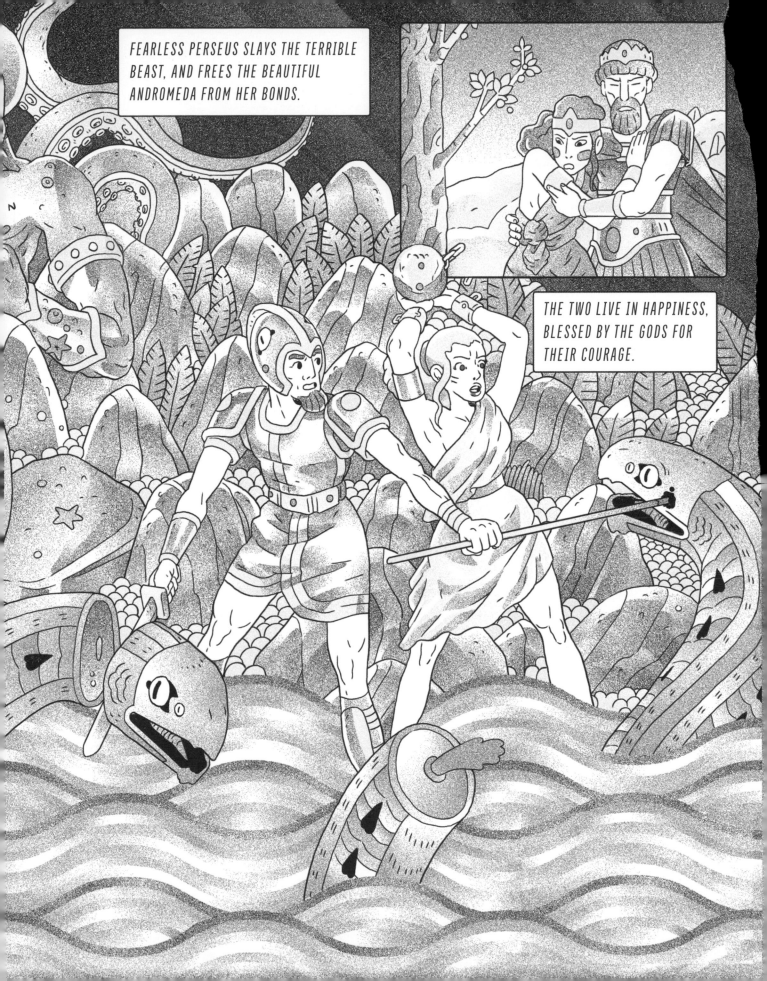

THE KING SETS HIM 10 TERRIBLE TASKS. AMONGST OTHERS, HE MUST DEFEAT THE HYDRA, KILL THE NEMEAN LION AND CAPTURE THE GIANT ERYMANTHIAN BOAR.

TO ATONE FOR THE SLAUGHTER OF HIS CHILDREN, HERCULES IS INSTRUCTED BY THE ORACLE TO SERVE THE EVIL KING EURYSTHEUS FOR 12 YEARS.

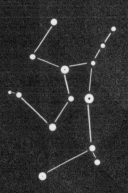

HERCULES

HERCULES WAS THE SON OF ALCMENE, A BEAUTIFUL WOMAN WHO WAS SEDUCED BY ZEUS. EVEN BEFORE HE WAS BORN, ZEUS'S WIFE, HERA, DESPISED HERCULES FOR THE EVIDENCE THAT HE PROVIDED OF HER HUSBAND'S DECEPTIONS. ATHENA, HOWEVER, TRICKED HERA INTO SUCKLING THE BABY HERCULES AND AS A RESULT HE BECAME SUPERNATURALLY POWERFUL AND STRONG. HERA WAS ENRAGED AND VOWED REVENGE UPON THE BOY.

HERCULES WAS FULLY GROWN BEFORE HERA FOUND A WAY TO ENSURE HIS SUFFERING EQUALLED HER OWN. DRIVEN MAD BY HERA'S SPELLS HERCULES SLAUGHTERED HIS OWN CHILDREN. RECOVERY BROUGHT DESPAIR AND GUILT SO POWERFUL THAT HE BEGGED THE ORACLE FOR A MEANS OF ATONEMENT.

THE ORACLE INSTRUCTED HERCULES TO SUBMIT TO HIS NEMESIS, KING EURYSTHEUS, AND SERVE HIM FOR 12 YEARS, WITH THE PROMISE THAT AT THE END OF THIS PERIOD, HE WOULD BE PURIFIED OF SIN AND BECOME IMMORTAL. HERCULES PUT HIS STRENGTH AND CUNNING TO GOOD USE, COMPLETING TEN LABOURS SET BY THE KING; HE KILLED AND SKINNED THE NEMEAN LION, DEFEATED THE MULTI-HEADED HYDRA AND DESTROYED THE MARAUDING BIRDS OF STYMPHALUS. ON COMPLETING HIS TENTH TASK HERCULES RETURNED TO MYCENAE, EXPECTING THE KING TO RELEASE HIM FROM HIS LABOURS, BUT THE DECEPTIVE KING SET TWO FURTHER TASKS; HERCULES WAS COMMANDED TO STEAL THE GOLDEN APPLES FROM HERA'S OWN GARDEN AND FINALLY FETCH CERBERUS, THE THREE-HEADED WATCHDOG OF HADES, TO MYCENAE.

WITH ONE FINAL EFFORT, HERCULES COMPLETED BOTH THESE TASKS, FORCING EURYSTHEUS TO RELEASE HIM. ZEUS WAS SO PROUD OF HIS SON THAT HE COMMEMORATED HIM IN THE STARS IN THE FORM OF A KNEELING MAN, TRIUMPHANT BUT EXHAUSTED BY HIS LABOURS.

STILL NOT SATISFIED, THE KING SETS TWO MORE TASKS. UPON THEIR COMPLETION, HERCULES IS AT LAST RELEASED FROM HIS SERVITUDE AND MADE IMMORTAL.

PEGASUS IS TAMED BY THE HERO BELLEROPHON AND HELPS HIS NEW MASTER KILL THE MIGHTY CHIMERA.

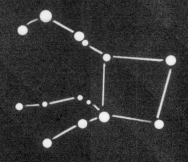

PEGASUS

WHEN PERSEUS CHOPPED OFF THE HEAD OF THE GORGON MEDUSA, A WINGED STALLION CALLED PEGASUS WAS BORN FROM HER NECK. USING A BRIDLE STOLEN FROM ATHENA, A GREAT HERO CALLED BELLEROPHON TAMED THE HORSE, AND TOGETHER THEY FLEW OFF TO KILL THE TERRIFYING CHIMERA, A FIRE-BREATHING MONSTER. BELLEROPHON THRUST HIS LEAD-TIPPED SPEAR INTO THE JAW OF THE BEAST. WHEN IT BREATHED FIRE, THE LEAD MELTED DOWN ITS THROAT, SEARING ITS VITAL ORGANS.

HAILED AS A HERO BY THE PEOPLE, BELLEROPHON GREW PROUD AND BECAME CONVINCED THAT ONLY THE GODS COULD TRULY APPRECIATE HIS ACHIEVEMENTS. HE MOUNTED PEGASUS AND URGED THE STALLION TOWARDS OLYMPUS SO THAT HE COULD HAVE AN AUDIENCE WITH THE GODS. ENRAGED BY THE MORTAL'S ARROGANCE, ZEUS SENT A GADFLY TO BITE PEGASUS. THE WINGED HORSE BUCKED HIS RIDER OFF, AND BELLEROPHON FELL INGLORIOUSLY TO EARTH.

PEGASUS CONTINUED TO OLYMPUS ALONE, WHERE ZEUS STABLED HIM COMFORTABLY AND GAVE HIM THE TASK OF CARRYING HIS THUNDERBOLTS. AT THE END OF HIS LONG AND LOYAL SERVICE, ZEUS COMMEMORATED THE STALLION BY DEPICTING THE FLIGHT OF PEGASUS IN THE STARS.

BELLEROPHON'S PRIDE GETS THE BETTER OF HIM... HE RIDES UP TO OLYMPUS TO BRAG OF HIS ACHIEVEMENTS TO THE GODS.

A FURIOUS ZEUS SENDS A GADFLY TO BITE PEGASUS. BELLEROPHON IS BUCKED OFF AND PEGASUS CONTINUES HIS JOURNEY ALONE, LOYALLY SERVING OUT THE REST OF HIS DAYS IN THE STABLES OF THE GODS.

BITTEN BY A SNAKE, EURYDICE DIES AND HER SOUL IS TAKEN TO THE UNDERWORLD.

A GRIEF-STRICKEN ORPHEUS FOLLOWS HIS BRIDE, CHARMING CHARON AND CEREBRUS WITH HIS SAD MUSIC.

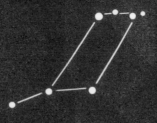

LYRA
(THE LYRE)

ORPHEUS WAS A FAMOUS POET AND MUSICIAN, WHOSE MUSIC ENCHANTED EVEN THE GOD APOLLO, WHO PRESENTED HIM WITH A HEAVENLY LYRE. WHEN ORPHEUS PLAYED THIS LYRE, IT WAS SAID THAT ROCKS WOULD ROLL AND TREES UPROOT TO FOLLOW THE SWEET NOTES OF HIS MUSIC.

ON HIS WEDDING DAY, A VENOMOUS SNAKE BIT ORPHEUS'S YOUNG WIFE, EURYDICE, AND SHE DIED. OVERCOME WITH GRIEF, ORPHEUS FOLLOWED HER TO THE UNDERWORLD. HIS MUSIC CHARMED THE FERRYMAN, CHARON, AND SOOTHED THE SNARLS OF THE THREE-HEADED GUARD DOG, CERBERUS. FINALLY HE STOOD BEFORE HADES, GOD OF THE UNDERWORLD, AND PLAYED A SONG SO MOURNFUL THAT HADES WAS MOVED TO PITY. HE AGREED THAT ORPHEUS COULD ESCORT HIS WIFE BACK TO THE WORLD OF THE LIVING UNDER ONE CONDITION; ORPHEUS WAS NOT TO LOOK BEHIND HIM UNTIL THEY HAD BOTH ARRIVED SAFELY UNDER THE LIGHT OF THE SUN.

ORPHEUS LED HIS WIFE UP THROUGH THE DARK PASSAGES, GUIDING HER BY THE SOUND OF HIS LYRE. AS THE SUNLIGHT REACHED HIM, HE FELT OVERCOME WITH JOY AND GLANCED BACK AT EURYDICE, BUT SHE HAD NOT YET EMERGED INTO THE LIGHT AND SO SHE WAS RETURNED TO THE UNDERWORLD, LOST TO ORPHEUS FOREVER.

ORPHEUS LIVED ALONE FOR THE REST OF HIS DAYS. APOLLO PLACED ORPHEUS'S LYRE AMONGST THE STARS IN COMMEMORATION OF HIS DIVINE MUSIC.

AS ORPHEUS BASKS IN THE FIRST RAYS OF SUNLIGHT, HE LOOKS BACK AT HIS WIFE - BUT IT IS TOO SOON - AND SHE IS LOST TO HIM FOREVER.

ALONE, ORPHEUS CONTINUES TO MAKE BEAUTIFUL MUSIC. APOLLO HONOURS HIS ART BY PLACING THE LYRE AMONGST THE STARS.

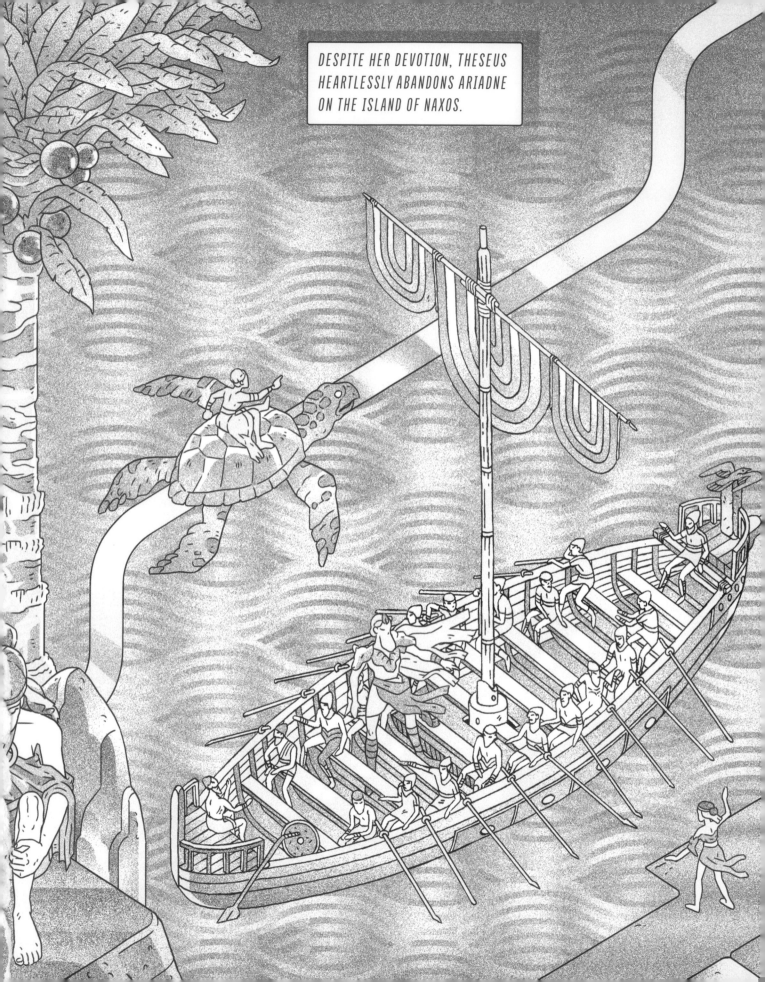

DESPITE HER DEVOTION, THESEUS HEARTLESSLY ABANDONS ARIADNE ON THE ISLAND OF NAXOS.

DIONYSUS COMES TO ARIADNE'S ASSISTANCE AND THE TWO FALL IN LOVE AND ARE MARRIED.

APHRODITE BLESSES THEIR UNION WITH A CROWN OF FIERY JEWELS. DIONYSUS FLINGS THE CROWN INTO THE HEAVENS TO COMMEMORATE THEIR LOVE FOREVER.

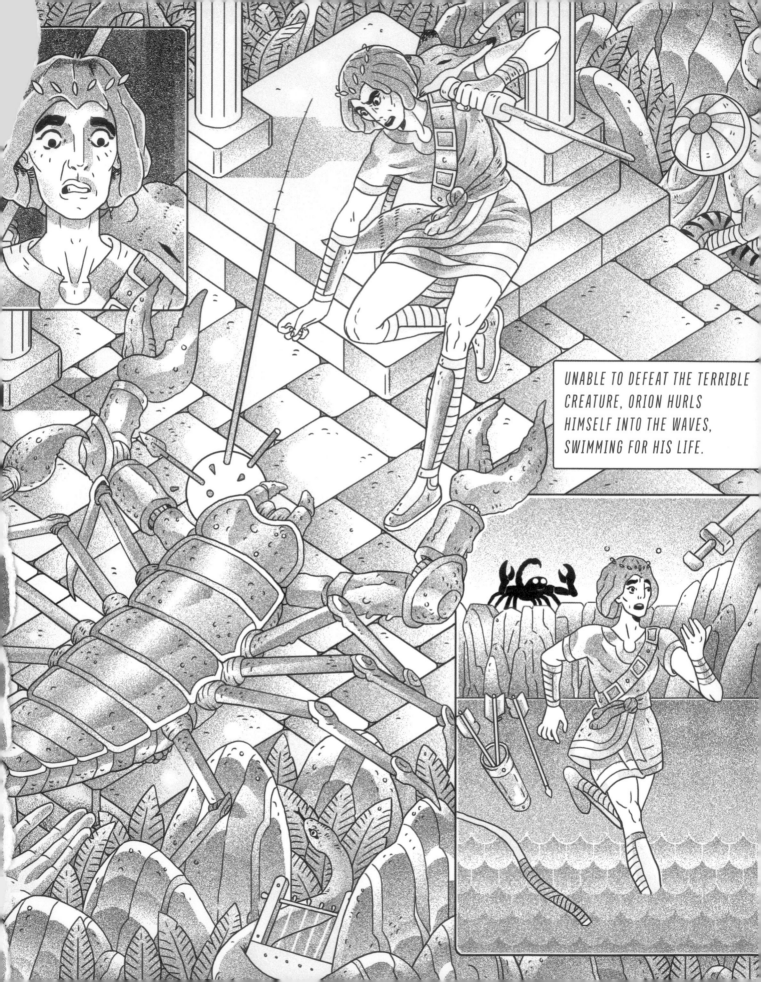

UNABLE TO DEFEAT THE TERRIBLE CREATURE, ORION HURLS HIMSELF INTO THE WAVES, SWIMMING FOR HIS LIFE.

ENRAGED BY THE BOASTS OF ORION, GAIA SENDS FORTH A MONSTROUS SCORPION TO PURSUE HIM TO THE ENDS OF THE EARTH.

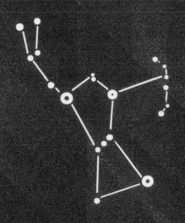

ORION AND SCORPIUS

ORION, THE HANDSOMEST MAN ALIVE, WAS FAMOUS FOR HIS HUNTING SKILLS. ARTEMIS, GODDESS OF THE HUNT, WAS SMITTEN WITH HIM AND TOOK HIM FOR HER HUNTING PARTNER. TO IMPRESS HER, HE BRAGGED THAT HE COULD KILL ANY CREATURE ON EARTH. GAIA, MOTHER EARTH, WAS OUTRAGED BY THIS BOAST, AND HER RAGE SHOOK THE MOUNTAINS, OPENING A HUGE CHASM FROM WHICH CLIMBED A MONSTROUS SCORPION.

ORION THREW HIS SHARPEST SPEAR AT THE BEAST, BUT IT SLID FROM THE SURFACE OF ITS HARD SHELL. THE SCORPION'S TAIL ARCHED FORWARD, ITS STING GLISTENING WITH POISON. SEEING NO ESCAPE, ORION RAN FOR THE BEACH AND FLUNG HIMSELF INTO THE WAVES. APOLLO, ARTEMIS'S BROTHER, WHO WAS JEALOUS OF HER AFFECTIONS FOR THE HUNTER, WAS WATCHING FROM ABOVE. HE CALLED FOR HIS SISTER AND POINTED OUT THE DISTANT FIGURE IN THE WATER, SAYING THAT THE SWIMMER HAD KILLED ONE OF HER FOREST PRIESTESSES. IN A FURY, ARTEMIS STRUNG HER BOW, AND WITH UNERRING ACCURACY, THE ARROW STRUCK ITS TARGET.

WHEN SHE REALISED WHAT SHE HAD DONE, ARTEMIS RAN TO RESCUE ORION, BUT IT WAS TOO LATE. GRIEF STRICKEN, SHE SET HIS FORM AMONG THE STARS NEXT TO HIS TWO FAITHFUL HOUNDS, CANIS MAJOR AND CANIS MINOR. BUT APOLLO, DETERMINED THAT ORION'S PUNISHMENT SHOULD BE REMEMBERED, PLACED THE SCORPION ON THE OPPOSITE SIDE OF THE SKY. EVERY WINTER ORION HUNTS IN THE SKY AND EVERY SUMMER HE FLEES AS THE CONSTELLATION OF THE SCORPION ARRIVES.

ARIADNE IS BESOTTED WITH THESEUS AND GIVES HIM A BALL OF STRING TO HELP HIM WITH HIS QUEST.

THESEUS SLAUGHTERS THE TERRIBLE MINOTAUR AND USES THE STRING TO RETRACE HIS STEPS THROUGH THE LABYRINTH.

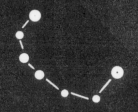

CORONA BOREALIS
(NORTHERN CROWN)

KING MINOS OFFENDED THE GOD POSEIDON BY REFUSING TO SACRIFICE A BEAUTIFUL WHITE BULL TO HIM. IN REVENGE, POSEIDON MADE MINOS'S WIFE, PASIPHAE, FALL IN LOVE WITH THE BULL, AND SHE SOON BECAME PREGNANT, GIVING BIRTH TO A MONSTROUS BEAST, HALF MAN AND HALF BULL; THE MINOTAUR. TO CONCEAL THIS EVIL BEING, THE KING ORDERED A LABYRINTH TO BE BUILT BENEATH HIS PALACE, SO COMPLEX THAT ESCAPE FROM ITS DARK AND TWISTING PASSAGES WOULD BE IMPOSSIBLE. WITHIN THE LABYRINTH THE MONSTER ROARED, SHAKING THE WALLS OF THE PALACE. YOUNG GIRLS WERE SACRIFICED TO CALM ITS RAGE AND THE PEOPLE LIVED IN DREAD THAT THEIR LOVED ONES WOULD BE NEXT. ONLY ARIADNE, THE KING'S DAUGHTER, WAS SAFE FROM SACRIFICE.

MANY BRAVE MEN DIED IN ATTEMPTS TO KILL THE MINOTAUR UNTIL THESEUS, HERO OF ATHENS, ARRIVED TO SEEK GLORY. ARIADNE FELL IN LOVE WITH HIM AT FIRST SIGHT. DESPERATE TO SAVE THE LIFE OF THIS HANDSOME HERO, ARIADNE GAVE THESEUS A BALL OF STRING, INSTRUCTING HIM TO UNRAVEL IT AS HE TRAVELLED THROUGH THE LABYRINTH, AND THEN USE IT TO RETRACE HIS STEPS. THESEUS FOLLOWED HER INSTRUCTIONS, SLAUGHTERED THE BEAST AND SUCCESSFULLY RETURNED TO DAYLIGHT, CLAIMING ARIADNE AS HIS BRIDE.

THE YOUNG COUPLE SET SAIL FOR ATHENS BUT HAD BARELY REACHED THE ISLAND OF NAXOS WHEN THESEUS TIRED OF HIS PRINCESS AND ABANDONED HER ON THE BEACH. THE GOD DIONYSUS CAME ACROSS THE BEREFT GIRL AND FELL IN LOVE WITH HER. THEIR MARRIAGE WAS BLESSED BY THE GODDESS APHRODITE, WHO PRESENTED ARIADNE WITH THE GIFT OF A BEAUTIFUL JEWEL-ENCRUSTED CROWN. OVERCOME WITH HAPPINESS, DIONYSUS FLUNG THE CROWN TOWARDS THE HEAVENS WHERE ITS JEWELS BECAME STARS.

APOLLO NEEDS SOME WATER FOR HIS FEAST, SO SENDS CORVUS THE CROW IN SEARCH OF A SPRING.

CORVUS
(THE CROW)

APOLLO, THE SUN GOD, WAS LOOKING TO HOST A FEAST IN HONOUR OF ZEUS. HOWEVER THE LAND WAS DRY AND SCORCHED AND THERE WAS NO WATER TO BE FOUND. HE GAVE A CHALICE TO CORVUS THE CROW, AND ORDERED THE BIRD TO FETCH SOME WATER. THE CROW FLEW OFF AND EVENTUALLY CAME ACROSS A SPRING. NEXT TO THE SPRING WAS A FIG TREE, LADEN WITH GREEN FRUIT. RATHER THAN FLYING STRAIGHT BACK TO HIS MASTER, CORVUS DALLIED, WAITING FOR THE FRUIT TO RIPEN.

A FEW DAYS PASSED, AND AFTER FEASTING, THE CROW REMEMBERED HIS ERRAND. FEARING THE WRATH OF APOLLO, HE PICKED UP A SNAKE AND RETURNED, GIVING THE EXCUSE THAT THE SNAKE HAD BLOCKED THE SPRING, AND PREVENTED HIM FROM FILLING THE CUP. BUT APOLLO, TALENTED IN THE ART OF PROPHECY, WAS NOT FOOLED AND CONDEMNED THE CROW TO A LIFE OF THIRST. AS A WARNING TO ALL NEVER TO DECEIVE THE GODS, APOLLO PUT THE CROW (CORVUS), THE CUP (CRATER) AND THE WATER SNAKE (HYDRA) IN THE SKY, WITH THE CUP JUST OUT OF REACH OF THE THIRSTY CROW.

ANGERED BY THE HOSPITALITY, THE CENTAURS ATTACK. HERCULES FIGHTS THEM OFF WITH A BARRAGE OF ARROWS.

PHOLUS OFFERS HERCULES SOME WINE.

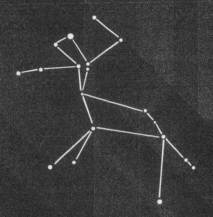

CENTAURUS
(THE CENTAUR)

THE CENTAURS WERE HALF MEN, HALF HORSES, RENOWNED FOR BEING ROWDY AND AGGRESSIVE CREATURES, DRINKING AND FIGHTING AT ANY OPPORTUNITY. CHIRON WAS DIFFERENT. A WISE AND GENTLE TEACHER AND HEALER, CHIRON THE CENTAUR EDUCATED YOUNG NOBLES IN HIS CAVE. ACHILLES AND HERCULES THE WARRIORS AND ASCLEPIUS THE HEALER ALL EXCELLED AS HIS PUPILS.

HERCULES PAID A VISIT TO THE CENTAURS ONE DAY, AND WAS OFFERED WINE BY A CENTAUR CALLED PHOLUS. THE OTHER CENTAURS WERE ENRAGED AT HAVING TO SHARE THEIR WINE AND ATTACKED HERCULES, WHO FOUGHT THEM OFF WITH A RAIN OF ARROWS. IN THE RESULTING FRACAS, CHIRON'S KNEE WAS PIERCED BY ONE OF HERCULES' ARROWS, WHICH WERE TIPPED WITH THE POISON OF THE HYDRA. TO HERCULES' HORROR, THE CENTAUR FELL TO THE FLOOR, WRITHING IN AGONY. BECAUSE HE WAS IMMORTAL, HE WOULD NOT DIE OF THE WOUND, BUT WOULD LIVE FOR ALL ETERNITY IN EXCRUCIATING PAIN. AFTER DAYS AND NIGHTS OF TERRIBLE SUFFERING, HERCULES BEGGED ZEUS FOR HELP.

ZEUS TRANSFERRED THE IMMORTALITY OF CHIRON TO PROMETHEUS, AND CHIRON WAS AT LAST ALLOWED TO DIE IN PEACE. ZEUS CAST THE IMAGE OF THE GREAT TEACHER INTO THE STARS.

SEIZING HANDFULS OF THE HERB, ASCLEPIUS ADMINISTERS IT TO THE BODY OF A DROWNED CHILD. THE BOY DRAWS BREATH, HIS LIFE RESTORED.

ASCLEPIUS, THE TALENTED HEALER, WATCHES IN AMAZEMENT AS A SNAKE REVIVES ITS DEAD COMPANION WITH A MAGIC HERB.

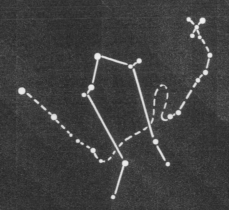

OPHIUCHUS
(THE SERPENT BEARER)

ASCLEPIUS, SON OF APOLLO, WAS TAKEN FROM HIS DYING MOTHER AND RAISED BY CHIRON THE CENTAUR AS IF HE WERE HIS OWN SON. CHIRON TAUGHT HIM THE HEALING ARTS, AND ASCLEPIUS EXCELLED AS A STUDENT, SURPASSING EVEN CHIRON HIMSELF.

ONE DAY, AS ASCLEPIUS WALKED BY THE RIVERBANK, HE DISCOVERED THE BODY OF A YOUNG BOY. SADDENED, HE SAT BESIDE THE BODY, MUSING ON THE TRAGEDY OF SUCH A SHORT LIFE, WHEN HIS EYE WAS CAUGHT BY A SNAKE SLITHERING TOWARDS THE RIVERBANK. DISGUSTED, HE CRUSHED THE SNAKE WITH HIS STAFF, AND WAS ABOUT TO TURN AWAY WHEN HE NOTICED A SECOND SNAKE GLIDING TOWARDS THE BODY OF THE FIRST. ASCLEPIUS WATCHED IN WONDER AS THE LIVING SNAKE PLACED A SPRIG OF HERBS ACROSS THE CRUSHED CORPSE, AND THE FIRST SNAKE SLOWLY RETURNED TO LIFE.

SEIZING HANDFULS OF THE MAGICAL HERB, ASCLEPIUS LIFTED THE BODY OF THE BOY AND, MIMICKING THE SNAKE, STROKED THE HERB GENTLY ACROSS HIS LIMBS. THE BOY DREW BREATH AND RETURNED TO THE LAND OF THE LIVING.

HADES, GOD OF THE UNDERWORLD, SAW THIS MIRACLE AND REALISED THAT THE FLOW OF DEAD SOULS WOULD CEASE IF THE POWERS OF THE MAGICAL HERB BECAME WIDELY KNOWN. HE REPORTED HIS CONCERNS TO ZEUS WHO, EQUALLY CONCERNED BY THE MORTAL'S POWER, STRUCK ASCLEPIUS DOWN WITH A THUNDERBOLT. APOLLO, ANGERED BY THE DEATH OF HIS GIFTED SON WAS EVENTUALLY APPEASED WHEN ZEUS GAVE ASCLEPIUS A NEW LIFE IN THE STARS AS THE SERPENT BEARER.